The Gingerbread Man

A little old woman made some gingerbread.
She cut out a man with a big round head.
She gave him a mouth and she gave him some eyes.
She put him in the oven – then what a surprise!

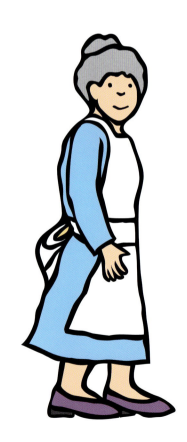

She went to the oven and opened the door.

The gingerbread man sprang onto the floor.

He ran from the cottage and down the lane.

The woman called, "Stop!" but all in vain.

The woman gave chase and led the race.

"Run, run, run, as fast as you can!"
 Sang the gingerbread man as he ran, ran, ran.
"Run, run, run, as fast as you can!
 You can't catch me, I'm the gingerbread man!"

The gingerbread man ran ever so fast.
A cow in a field saw him hurrying past.

"You look good to eat," said the cow. "Come back!"
But the gingerbread man ran away down the track.

The woman gave chase and led the race.
A curious cow followed them now.

"Run, run, run, as fast as you can!"
Sang the gingerbread man as he ran, ran, ran.
"Run, run, run, as fast as you can!
You can't catch me, I'm the gingerbread man!"

The gingerbread man ran ever so fast.
A horse by a tree saw him hurrying past.

"You look good to eat," said the horse. "Come back!"
But the gingerbread man ran away down the track.

The woman gave chase and led the race.
A curious cow followed them now.
A hungry horse galloped, of course.

"Run, run, run, as fast as you can!"
  Sang the gingerbread man as he ran, ran, ran.
"Run, run, run, as fast as you can!
  You can't catch me, I'm the gingerbread man!"

He came to a river and stood on the side.
He could not swim, and the river was wide.

Then a sly old fox came up and said,
"You can ride across on my tail instead."

The woman gave chase and led the race.
A curious cow followed them now.
A hungry horse galloped, of course.
A friendly fox swam round the rocks.

"Run, run, run, as fast as you can!"
  Sang the gingerbread man as he ran, ran, ran.
"Run, run, run, as fast as you can!
  You can't catch me, I'm the gingerbread man!"

"My feet are wet!" said the gingerbread man.
"Climb onto my back," said the fox, "if you can."

"They're still getting wet," said a voice in his ear.
"Climb onto my nose," said the fox, "right here."

The gingerbread man did just as he said,
The sly fox smiled and tossed his head.
He opened his mouth and … CRUNCH, CRUNCH, CRUNCH!
He had that gingerbread man for lunch.

"Run, run, run, as fast as you can!"
  Sang the gingerbread man as he ran, ran, ran.
"Run, run, run, as fast as you can!
  You can't catch me, I'm the gingerbread man!"

"Run, run, run, as fast as you can!"
  Sang the gingerbread man as he ran, ran, ran.
"Run, run, run, as fast as you can!"
  The sly old fox ate the gingerbread man!